Anderson Elementary
Library

TWENTY AND TEN
by Claire Huchet Bishop
Illustrated by William Pène du Bois


"The Nazis are looking for those children," said Sister Gabriel. "If we take them we must never let on that they are here. Never. Even if we are questioned. We can never betray them, no matter what they do to us. Do you understand?"

During the German occupation of France, twenty French children are sent to a refuge in the mountains with the wise Sister Gabriel. When ten Jewish children are brought to the school, hiding them seems like a game—until Nazi soldiers arrive, and ten lives depend on the courage and cunning of twenty.

*Twenty and Ten* is based on a true story—only one of many incidents that took place all over the country during the Second World War. It is a story that has much to say to children of any age.

by *Claire Huchet Bishop*
as told by *Janet Joly*

Illustrated by
*William Pène du Bois*

L 4.0
P 2.0

# TWENTY AND TEN

Anderson Elementary
Library

*Puffin Books*

PUFFIN BOOKS
Published by the Penguin Group
A division of Penguin Books USA Inc.,
375 Hudson Street, New York, New York 10014, U.S.A.
Penguin Books Ltd, 27 Wrights Lane, London W8 5TZ England
Penguin Books Australia Ltd, Ringwood, Victoria, Australia
Penguin Books Canada Ltd, 10 Alcorn Avenue, Toronto, Ontario, Canada M4V 3B2
Penguin Books (N.Z.) Ltd, 182–190 Wairau Road, Auckland 10, New Zealand

Penguin Books Ltd, Registered Offices: Harmondsworth, Middlesex, England

First published in 1991 by Viking Penguin, a division of Penguin Books USA Inc.

First published by The Viking Press 1952
Published in Puffin Books 1978
24   26   28   30   29   27   25

Copyright 1952 by Claire Huchet Bishop and William Pène du Bois
Copyright © renewed 1980 by Claire Huchet Bishop and William Pène du Bois
All rights reserved

Library of Congress Cataloging in Publication Data
Bishop, Claire Huchet.    Twenty and ten.
Summary: Twenty school children hide ten Jewish chil-
dren from the Nazis occupying France during World War II.
[1. World War, 1935–1945—Jews—Fiction.   2. France—
History—German occupation, 1940–1945—Fiction]
I. Du Bois, William Pène.   II. Title.
PZ7.B5245Tw 1978   [Fic]   77-12730
ISBN 0 14 03.1076 2

Printed in the United States of America

Set in Garamond

Except in the United States of America, this book is sold subject
to the condition that it shall not, by way of trade or otherwise,
be lent, re-sold, hired out, or otherwise circulated without the
publisher's prior consent in any form of binding or cover other
than that in which it is published and without a similar
condition including this condition being imposed on
the subsequent purchaser.

To Blanche Marsay

because of

our lasting mutual affection

# Contents

# TWENTY AND TEN

# 1. Make-Believe

It all started when we were playing at The Flight into Egypt. Make-believe. It was in the schoolyard, at recess time, right after the Christmas vacation, beginning of the year 1944.

I have to write all about it now, lest I forget later on, the way most grownups do forget the very important things, such as not talking about a treasure or not asking what one is thinking about. If I write now all I remember about "it," perhaps when I am old, let us say twenty, somebody may find these pages and make a book. But that is a very long way off: I am only thirteen, and I was eleven when "it" happened.

My name is Janet. There were also George and Philip and Henry and Denise and Louis and many others. Twenty in all. And we were all fifth-graders except Louis, who was only four years old but was allowed to be with us because he was Denise's little brother. And this was permitted because the war was on and France was occupied, and the children were herded all together where it was safest for them to be. In our town the boys' school and the girls' school were combined and each grade was sent somewhere in the country.

We, the fifth-graders, boys and girls, were given that lovely old house on the top of a mountain. It was called Beauvallon, Beautiful Valley, because we could see the valley for miles and miles from up there, and it was very beautiful.

Anyway, we were all up there, the fifth-graders and Louis, and Sister Gabriel was with us, and we were very happy because we just loved her. She was young and gay and quick. She never walked, she flew.

Now, as I was saying at the very beginning, we were playing at The Flight into Egypt. I was Mary, and George was Joseph, and Louis was the little one.

The other boys and girls asked, "And who are *we* going to be?"

I said, "The Egyptians, of course. Can't you see? The three of us, Joseph, the little one, and myself, we are DPs, refugees, Jewish refugees. We have fled into Egypt."

"Why?" asked Denise.

"Because King Herod wanted to kill the little one. Don't you remember? Sister Gabriel told us all about it," I said proudly.

"What do we Egyptians do?" asked Philip.

Then it was that Henry said flatly, "We sell."

"Sell?" I cried.

"Well, what do you think?" went on Henry. "Jewish refugees have got to eat, just like the others, don't they?"

I didn't know what to say because I didn't want to make

· 12 ·

Henry angry. He is so very good at make-believe games. Also, it was really because of him that I was Mary. Joseph, I mean George, said he did not want a fair Mary. He said it was all wrong, since Mary was dark. And I was furious, because I knew all the time he said that because he prefers Denise, who is dark. So I said Mary *was* a blond, and the proof was that I had seen a picture of her made by a man called Memling, and she did have blond hair in that picture.

Then Henry stepped in and said, "George is right, and Janet is right too, because sometimes Mary is dark and sometimes she is fair. Mary can be French, Spanish, Russian, Negro, Indian, Chinese, anything, anything at all."

Denise said, "How do you know?"

And Henry said, "I know." And that was that, because Henry is very, very clever. Then he added that since we had had a dark Mary for the Nativity (Denise), we could have a fair one for The Flight into Egypt, and I could be Mary. (Henry does like me.)

"Don't you think it is only just?" asked Henry grandly.

George nodded; he could hardly do anything else.

So I was Mary, and I didn't want to make Henry mad. When he suggested that the Egyptians had to sell to the Holy Family because refugees have got to eat, I had to think very fast for an answer.

"Henry is right," I said cautiously. "All refugees have got to eat. My idea was that we—the little one, Joseph, and myself—we would make the journey first." I pointed to the whole playground. "Then when we get to Egypt, you Egyptians *give* us everything: the baker bread, the butcher meat, the housewives diapers for the little one—"

"Phew," interrupted Henry, "that's no fun. What is the matter with Joseph anyway?" he asked, turning toward Joseph-George and getting right into the game as he knew so well how to do. "Can't you pay for the stuff, Mr. Joseph?"

" 'Course," said Joseph. "I can work. I am a carpenter."

"Look, fellow," said Henry, "already there are not enough jobs to go around in this village."

"Henry!" I stamped my foot, I was almost cross. "Henry, you cannot talk to Joseph that way, to *Joseph!*"

"Be quiet," ordered Henry. "Are we playing or not?"

"Yes, of course. I guess I'm just stupid. Go ahead. Only," I added, "don't make it too long, because Louis, I mean Jesus, is awfully heavy in my arms. I think that all you Egyptians could at least offer me a chair."

Philip made the gesture of pushing a chair toward me, and I thanked him.

"All right," said Henry, "now we men can talk this over. Mr. Joseph, what about your ration cards?"

"We don't have any," answered Joseph.

"That's bad," mused Henry, stroking an imaginary beard.

"But, as I told you," retorted Joseph, "I can work."

"Not so fast, not so fast," admonished Henry. "I already

· 14 ·

Anderson Elementary Library

told you: work is no good. And now you have no ration cards."

"We've got to eat," went on Joseph doggedly.

"Sure, sure," said Henry. Then he dropped his voice. "But you have got money, haven't you?"

"Henry!" wailed Denise. (She was very sentimental.)

"Don't butt in," snapped Henry. "I know what I'm saying. That Mr. Joseph is trying to get work away from us Egyptians. And he has no ration cards. And he pretends he has no money, but he is double-crossing us, because, as a matter of fact, he is rich."

We all said, "Oh!" We were petrified. (That means

William Pène du Bois

turned into stones.) And Louis, I mean Jesus, in my arms, started to cry. Then I was really cross and I shrieked, "See what you have done! Now the little one is crying. You are horrid, Henry, horrid! Everyone knows that the Holy Family was very poor!"

"Is that so?" queried Henry as cool as could be. "Well, what about that myrrh, frankincense, and gold the Wise Men brought them? That's worth a lot. What about it, Mr. Joseph?"

Everybody was quiet, quiet. We were just holding our breath and waiting for Joseph-George's answer. But it did not come. Joseph-George only looked crestfallen. So I had to speak up.

"Dear Joseph," I said tenderly, "you are so unpractical. Just as when we went up to Bethlehem for the census and you had made no hotel reservation in advance. Now, what do you think happened to the Wise Men's gifts? All gone, of course. How could we have taken that long journey and come this far without paying our way through? I have handed over our treasures right and left. And now I have nothing: not a bit of myrrh, not a grain of frankincense, not a mite of gold. See—hold the little one a minute please—" And I got up and gave Joseph the little one.

Then I turned my pockets inside out, and I shook my dress, and I cried, "Look, Egyptians! Nothing! Nothing!"

"It's a trick!" announced Henry.

I hardly knew what happened next, it happened so fast. Joseph-George put down the little one quickly, glaring at *me,* of all people, with blazing eyes. Then he marched toward Henry with closed fists, muttering, "Unpractical! A trick! Money! Ration cards! Work! I'll show you!"

And suddenly we were all fighting like cats and dogs. Some of us on George's side and others on Henry's, but soon we did not know which was which. It was a regular free-for-all, the boys pummeling one another and the girls pulling one another's hair.

The soft white wings of Sister Gabriel's headdress flapped hurriedly across the yard.

"There, there, children!" she called. "Shame on you! No, I don't want to hear about a thing. Think of you getting into a fight when I was just coming to tell you—"

"What? What?" we cried eagerly, crowding around her.

"You will see. In the classroom. Quick. Now you shake hands with one another and file in on tiptoe."

We did. In the classroom a young man sat on a chair. He looked very tired. He was not shaved. His clothes were covered with dust. We slipped noiselessly to our benches and waited in dead silence until Sister Gabriel made a sign with her head for the young man to speak.

When he opened his mouth his voice had a croak, as it does when one has not slept. "Boys and girls," he said, "I have to speak to you just as if you were adults. You know

that the Germans occupy France. You know also about the refugees and the DPs?" We nodded. "Now, do you know that there are people who not only are refugees and DPs but have absolutely no place to go, because if the Nazis find them they will kill them?"

A shiver ran through the class.

"Do you know who those people are?" asked the young man.

You could have heard a pin drop, and we were amazed when we saw George raising his hand. He got up and said, "The Jews."

We had no idea what he was talking about, but the young man looked very startled and asked, "How did you know?"

George became very excited and shrieked, "Because there was Herod, and the Egyptians, and I was Joseph, and—"

He was all red and confused and he dropped to his seat and hid his head in his arms. We almost burst out laughing, but we did not dare because the young man was very serious and sad. To our surprise he said, "That boy is right. It is the same story—always—throughout the centuries. This time Herod's soldiers are the Nazis. That's all."

He waited a little while, then he asked quietly, "Boys and girls, do you know what happened when Jesus' family was hunted by Herod's soldiers?"

We all sang out at once, "They fled into Egypt."

"Yes," said the young man, "and they remained hidden

there, did they not? Now, once more, Jesus' family is hunted and will be killed if we do not hide them. Will you, boys and girls, help? Will you take with you, here, and hide, ten Jewish boys and girls whose fathers and mothers are dead already?"

Of course we all cried, "Yes! Yes!" We were absolutely thrilled. This was not make-believe any more. It was the real thing.

Sister Gabriel spoke up, "I did not expect less from you boys and girls. But you must understand what this means. The Nazis are looking for those children. If we take them we must never let on that they are here. Never. Even if we are questioned. We can never betray them, no matter what the Nazis do to us. Do you understand?"

Well, of course! Had we not played at being the Egyptians? By then, anyway, we could hardly wait to see the new children. And we were delighted when the young man turned to Sister Gabriel and said, "They are hiding in the woods now. We have walked all night. May I bring them in?"

Sister Gabriel nodded.

The young man went over to her; he took her hand and touched his forehead with it, bowing at the same time, and he said, "You know that *you* can be shot for this?"

Sister Gabriel smiled quietly. "Bring them in quickly," she said. "They must be so tired."

# 2. Gold

There was just time for the Jewish children to get washed before the lunchbell rang, and it was in the dining room that we saw them first. There were a few of them sitting at each table so that we all could have a chance of getting acquainted.

As we filed in Philip said, "What's the fuss about? They look just like us. Nazis are crazy!"

"What do I smell?" chanted Henry, sniffing. "Leek and potato soup!" He smacked his lips and rubbed his stomach. "My favorite! My, am I hungry!"

"So am I," said George.

"I collapse," announced Philip, imitating a rag doll.

I said, "There is not nearly enough to eat with those ration cards. I wish it were like *before*. My older brother told me all about it. He said that *before* he had so much to eat that sometimes he could not finish. He actually left something on his plate!"

"Don't make up stories," whined Denise, holding Louis by the hand. Louis started to jump up and down. "I want to eat up to here"—he pointed to his throat—"up to here, just once, just once!"

"Quiet!" said Henry impatiently, turning to us. "Look at the bowls! What is the matter? There is even less than usual. Something is wrong."

"Children!" called Sister Gabriel as we reached our places. "You probably have already noticed that there is less soup than usual in your bowls. Let me explain. We have ten new boys and girls. They have no ration cards."

"Can they get them tomorrow?" asked Philip.

"No," said Sister Gabriel, "they cannot. They can never

ask for any ration cards, because if they do the Nazis will find out where they are."

George said, "How can they eat without ration cards?"

"They will die," said Henry matter of factly.

"That's right," went on Sister Gabriel. "Unless we share with them our own ration cards. That is what we are doing today. That is why there is less soup for each one of us. From now on the slogan is: *We all eat, or nobody eats.*"

We sat down in silence. We did not feel like talking. Soon we could tell by the very sound of the spoons that everybody was getting to the bottom of each bowl pretty quickly—too quickly.

Henry sat across the table from me. He was counting the spoonfuls and swallowing very slowly to make it last: nine, ten. . . . He sighed, and I heard him mutter to himself, "Perhaps three more." He threw a glance at his new neighbor, who had already cleaned his bowl. He was a small blond boy, doubled up on his chair, and he had large dark circles under his eyes.

"What's your name?" asked Henry in a low voice.

"A—A—Arthur," said the boy.

"I am Henry. Look, Arthur. Do me a favor. Eat the rest of my soup."

Arthur shook his head vehemently.

Henry compressed his lips and said, "Please. To tell you the truth, I hate the stuff."

Quickly I put my hand on my mouth: I was going to scream. Didn't I know how fond of that soup Henry was, and what an appetite he had?

Arthur's eyes became very large, as if he were about to cry, and before he could say a word Henry had emptied his bowl in the other's and, breathing hard, had sat back in his chair, looking straight in front of him. I was speechless. Presently Arthur finished the soup. Then I saw him fumble in his pocket and slip something into Henry's hand under the table. "For you," he said. "A woman gave it to me on the road last night."

"No," said Henry, and he too shook his head vehemently.

"Yes," went on Arthur quietly. "Can you guess what it is?"

I could tell that Henry was trying to feel under the table

without looking. Suddenly I saw his face relax and beam with pleasure. "Thanks, pal," he said.

Of course I was dying of curiosity, and I was so glad that right after lunch Henry came over to me in the yard and said, "Now, we are real Egyptians, aren't we?"

"Is that why you gave Arthur your soup?" I asked.

"How did you guess?" Henry smiled.

"Oh!" sneered Denise, who had overheard us. "Henry just wants to show off. This morning he was the one who tried to sell goods to the Holy Family. To sell! And now—did you by any chance get myrrh, frankincense, or gold in return for your soup?" she mocked.

"Mind your own business!" barked Henry. "Anyway, you have no idea how I was going to end the game this morning if I had been free to do so. Besides—" He stopped and seemed to make a big discovery. "As a matter of fact," he went on slowly, "I did get something back. Gold. Pure gold."

"Oh, show us! Show us!" Denise and I both cried. But he would not.

It was only in the evening when it was already somewhat dark that Henry made a sign for me to follow him. And there, behind a big tree, he showed me Arthur's gift. I put my two hands on my chest: it was a small piece of chocolate! We had not seen any for months and months, and, surely, Arthur had not either. It was a priceless gift.

I could not possibly ask Henry to let me have a taste. Such

a precious thing! And, after all, it did belong to Henry. He had earned it. So my heart leaped when I heard him say, "Wet your finger in your mouth."

I knew right away what he was up to. I did it. Then he took hold of my wet finger and ran it back and forth, back and forth, on the piece of chocolate. "Suck your finger now," he said. I did. And I kept doing it for a long time after I had licked all the chocolate off of it. Henry bit off a piece of the chocolate about half the size of a pea and ate it. We did not speak. We were very quiet.

Then Henry said, "If we are careful it will last a long time."

He said "we," so it meant he was thinking to let me have another turn sometime. But I did not let on at all for fear he might change his mind if I did. Yet I had to protect "our gold" as much as possible and I said, "Henry, aren't you afraid it will melt in your pocket?"

"Didn't think of it," said Henry. "Of course there is paper around it. Nevertheless, you are right. Besides, Sister Gabriel might find it, and there would be all sorts of questions. Guess we'll have to eat it all, right now."

"Never in your life!" I said, gasping. "It's a treasure. What about hiding it somewhere? A place only you and I will know about?"

"Right," said Henry. "Come on quickly before anybody misses us. I know a place."

We raced behind the house. There the hill starts to go up abruptly. It is covered with thicket, brush, and is very stony. It is real wild country, and I would have been afraid there at twilight if Henry had not gone ahead. We came to the brook that trickles down the slope, among rocks and boulders. Henry stopped and bent over. He took out a slab of rock from the side of the bank. This left a clean, cool, sandy hole. In it we laid the piece of chocolate, and we closed the "safe" again with the slab.

I whispered, "How are we ever going to find it again?"

"Look," said Henry, "it just faces that triangular stone in midstream."

"Henry," I promised, "I will never come here without you."

After that we ran back as fast as we could. But, all of a sudden, Henry grasped my wrist. I stood still. As I did so I heard a noise such as we had made when our feet kicked the stones while we ran. Only, this time, *we* were not making it. Then it died out, and we went on down, Henry not letting go of my hand.

Back in the schoolyard, and as we were going into the house, I asked softly, "What was it? Perhaps just the echo of our own footsteps?"

"No," whispered Henry, slowly shaking his head. "I think it was somebody."

# 3. The Cave

Next day, at recess time, as he went past me Henry whispered, "Go up there and wait for me." Of course I knew what he meant, and, when no one was looking, I went around the house and raced up the hill. It was bright sunshine, and I was not afraid. I found the place with the triangular stone in midstream and I sat down and waited. I was not going to open the safe without Henry. I waited and waited, and I began to feel a little uneasy. Once or twice I thought I heard a noise. So I was much relieved when Henry came up. Arthur was with him. "I brought him," said Henry. "I think he should be in with us on this." I was glad. I liked Arthur.

So we all three knelt, and Henry very carefully removed the slab. Without looking inside the safe he said to Arthur, "You have the first look."

Arthur did. He did not say a word.

"What do you think of our safe?" I asked. "Isn't it a grand hiding place?"

Still Arthur did not say a word.

"Take it out, Arthur," Henry said. "After all, it was *your* treasure first."

Arthur raised his head and looked at us. His face was all pinched, as if he had closed it shut, and he said in a choking voice, "There's nothing there."

"Nothing!" Henry and I gasped, and we bumped our heads trying to look into the hole, both of us at the same time. Arthur was right: there was nothing there. The piece of chocolate, our gold, was gone.

"Who could—" started Henry, and then we three jumped, because we heard the noise of stones kicked by footsteps, and I saw something blue behind a bush and then it disappeared. "There! There! Catch her!" I screamed. I knew at once it was Denise.

We all started in that direction. And, sure enough, it was Denise, but though we ran as fast as we could, she was way ahead of us, and she kept leaping like a goat, always out of reach.

Suddenly she shrieked, moved her arms frantically, and disappeared as if swallowed by the earth. When, all out of breath, we came to the spot where we had seen her last, she was nowhere. We looked and looked around. Then we started to call:

"Denise! Denise! Don't hide! Come out! We have got you! Come on!"

From far away we heard a tiny voice, "Come here and get me. I'm hurt."

"Where are you?" we called.

"Right here, in the cave."

"The cave?" we exclaimed. "There is no cave."

"There is," said Denise's voice. "Right under that boulder where you stand. That's where I slipped and fell into
the cave."

We went all around, trying to find the entrance to the

cave, but we could not see anything, and all the while we could hear Denise sobbing underneath.

It was Arthur who solved the riddle. At the bottom of the boulder there was a crack. We had paid no attention to it because it was much too small for anyone to go through it. But, as a matter of fact, it could be done—that is what Arthur discovered. You only had to place yourself in a certain position, and if you did, your body fitted the bumps and angles of the crack and you could slip through, which was what had happened by accident to Denise.

Arthur already had his legs through when Henry pulled him back, saying, "Just a minute. Listen, Denise, we are coming to your rescue under one condition: you give us back the treasure. If not, you can just stay down there and rot." (Henry can be harsh sometimes.)

"I promise! I promise!" wailed Denise.

Then Arthur went down. We heard him say, "Isn't this something! Henry, come down!"

"Is there room for me too?" I called.

"Sure," said Arthur.

So Henry and I slipped down the crack. And, lo and behold! we found ourselves in a natural underground cave, very spacious, with a dry, sandy floor. At least fifteen people could have stood in that cave. It was such a marvelous discovery that we nearly forgot about Denise, who lay there whimpering. Arthur remembered first and went over to her.

But Henry said, "Just a minute, Arthur. Denise, the treasure first."

Denise gave Arthur the chocolate, and of course we could see that she had nibbled a little piece out of our gold, but it was fortunate that she had not swallowed it whole. So we did not say anything. Besides, she was badly frightened and we were too excited about the cave.

"It's a marvelous place," commented Henry, looking around. "We shouldn't say anything to Sister Gabriel. It has to be a secret."

He looked down at Denise and seemed suddenly to make up his mind about something. "Let's sit down and celebrate," he said. "Let's all, the four of us, eat up the treasure now."

Denise's eyes shone. "Cross my heart," she said, "I won't tell anyone about 'our' cave. And I am sorry. I really didn't want to eat the treasure all by myself. I wanted one lick. I haven't had any chocolate for so long. I just wanted a taste. One lick. Like Janet had."

Then we knew for sure that she had spied on us and that it had been her footsteps we had heard the evening before. And I knew that she had wanted that lick so badly, not only because, like the rest of us, she had not tasted chocolate for so long, but also because *I* had had one lick, and she was jealous that Henry had shared the gold with *me*. But I didn't say anything because she was truly sorry, and she was hurt,

and also I kept thinking that if Henry had chosen her instead of me, I would have been so mad that I might have done worse than Denise did.

Arthur summed up everything nicely. "Let us all be friends."

We shook hands, and the four of us ate the treasure, very, very slowly, one tiny bit each, in turn.

Then Arthur went up again to see if the coast was clear.

Henry took Denise by the shoulders and I by the feet, and we lifted her through the crack. Arthur grabbed her and pulled her out. Then I hoisted myself through. Henry came up last.

Denise said she could not walk, and we were very annoyed because it meant we would have to carry her and Sister Gabriel would discover what had happened.

Henry became quite cross. "You would spoil our plan, wouldn't you?" he told Denise reproachfully. "Helpless! Always helpless one way or another! I cannot stand a girl who—"

But Arthur put himself between them and said very gently to Denise, though I could see he too was annoyed, "Just try to put your foot down. Lean on me. Just try."

"I can't!" wailed Denise.

"Just try," Arthur went on with that encouraging and at the same time very determined tone of voice. "Here, Henry, help her on the other side. Now take it easy, Denise. We won't let you go."

Denise did as Arthur told her, and suddenly her face brightened. She could put her foot down. And she found out that she *could* walk. She had been a little bruised and very frightened.

We all came back to Beauvallon very happy, and, as we crossed the yard, Henry put a finger on his lips and said, *"Motus,"* which is the French word for "mum."

# 4. The Real Thing

The third day after the arrival of the new children we were all friends and did not think any more who was what, when suddenly, at lunchtime, we almost had a quarrel. The new children insisted on giving us back some of their share of food, and we wanted to give them something from our own plates.

Sister Gabriel said, "Boys and girls, all plates are alike, and you should eat just what is in front of you. That's all."

When we went out Philip said, "I don't like it. We have to do something about this."

Henry said, "Let's have a meeting."

So we all gathered together. Philip explained, "My point is this: I like to eat fairly well once in a while"— Philip is very tall and large—"and I like my buddies to eat fairly well once in a while too. So I suggest we take turns, one person at each meal passing his plate all around the table and the rest of us sharing a little off our own plates. That will make quite a meal, and by and by everyone in turn will come to have almost his fill for once. How is that?"

"Grand," said Arthur. "Only do you think that Sister Gabriel will let us do that? She didn't seem to approve of anything this noon except eating just what had been placed before us."

"Oh," said I, "you don't know Sister Gabriel yet. She understands everything. We have but to explain. Here she is. Let us ask her."

But we never had a chance, because Sister Gabriel spoke first. "Boys and girls," she said, "I have to go down to the village." (Dieulefit is the name, which means "God-made-it"— I can't help it, it *is* the name.) "I haven't called at the post office for two weeks. There may be letters, and even some food packages for some of you in which we can all share. We need that extra very badly. So I have to go. Now listen. I won't be long. It is a three-mile walk. That makes six miles both ways. Of course it will take a little longer coming up again, but I should make it in about three hours and a half. It is one-thirty now. I should be back around five, before it gets really dark. Can you stay here all by yourselves and behave as you did the other times?"

We said "Yes" right away. We—that is, all but the new children—were used to that arrangement. About every fortnight Sister Gabriel went to Dieulefit to get the mail and packages. We always managed nicely all by ourselves while she was gone. That's what happens when there is what grownups call "an emergency." Then people, especially children, can do things they never would have done before. Sister Gabriel knew that she could trust us.

But George, looking very worried, spoke up, "Sister, what about Herod's soldiers, the Nazis?"

A shadow crossed Sister Gabriel's face. "That is in the hand of God," she said. "However, don't worry about it. If I go now it is precisely because I have heard, grapevine fashion, that the Nazis have all left the neighborhood and are very busy hunting for people on the other side of the Rhône River, fifty miles from here. Otherwise I would not go. And I won't be long. So now, be good. There are thirty slices of bread cut in the kitchen, and thirty apples!"

"Apples!" we shrieked.

"Yes, it is a surprise. You can have a picnic."

After she was gone we did not do anything for quite a long time. We watched the white wings of her headdress getting smaller and smaller on the road, while the large empty basket she carried kept swinging in the crook of her arm.

When she had disappeared Philip said, "What about having that picnic right now and getting it over with?"

We all liked the idea. In those days we had so little to eat that we were ready to start all over again right after a meal. So we went into the kitchen and we brought out the bread and the apples and we ate it all. I say we, the thirty of us. If I don't speak about everyone it is only because it would take too much time. Also, it happened that some of us had more ideas than others, and they are the ones I remember best. But the thirty of us were in "it," right straight through, all together. We could not have done "it" any other way.

After we were through the picnic George said, "What about playing at The Flight into Egypt again? Arthur could be Joseph."

Well, I suppose George was rather fed up with being Joseph, especially because of what had taken place the last time. Only his offering Arthur the part made it impossible for me to be Mary again. That is, I too had to offer to give up my part. That made me mad, not only because I liked to be Mary, but because if I were to give up my part I wanted to do so all by myself, and not be pushed into it, so to speak, by somebody else.

So I said casually, "No, George, you make an excellent Joseph." (I felt ashamed because George looked so pleased. George is really nice though he is stubborn.) "But," I went on, "*I* don't have to be Mary. Suzanne could be."

Suzanne was one of the new little girls. She always seemed scared and unhappy. I had been looking after her a bit, and I did think that playing a part might cheer her up, only I didn't know if she would like it or not.

"What about it, Suzanne?" I asked, putting my arm around her.

At once Suzanne brightened up and said eagerly, "I know how to be Mary. I was Mary back home, at the library, L'Heure Joyeuse, in Paris."

"Splendid!" cried George at once. He did not speak any more of giving up his part: Suzanne has dark hair. And though I was sorry not to be Mary again, yet I was the only one who had given up a part, which was what I wanted.

Everybody was pleased. George came forward and took Suzanne by the hand. He seemed all excited, not at all as he had been when I was Mary, and he announced that we Egyptians were to gather at the bottom of the garden slope, because the Holy Family would start the journey from "Galilee," at the top of the slope and go "way down in Egypt land."

Suzanne asked, "What about the donkey?"

"She is right," said Henry. "We never thought of it before. What about it, Philip?"

Philip is much bigger than any of us. He is from Normandy, and there people are large and blond and they shave as Americans do. Of course Philip did not shave. Not yet!

"Fine," he said with his usual bright smile. He bent his back, and Suzanne climbed on his shoulders. Then I put Louis, the little one, in George's arms, I mean Joseph's, because I thought Philip had enough to carry for the time being. I said to Suzanne—I mean Mary, "You can always take Jesus in your arms when you rest on the road."

Then all of us Egyptians ran down to the bottom of the slope. We could see the Holy Family up there. And right away we were delighted with Suzanne's acting: she turned her head partly around, she shaded her eyes with her hand and looked far down the valley behind her.

"Good," said Henry. "She's looking for Herod's soldiers."

"They're coming! They're coming!" shrieked Suzanne.

"She *is* good," approved Henry placidly.

We all called, "Quick! Come down into Egypt! Quick!"

While we were still waving we saw Suzanne slip off Philip's back and run toward us at top speed. She tumbled into the midst of us, shaking from head to foot. "They're coming! They're coming!" she yelled. And suddenly Philip and George were also among us, panting. "They're coming! They're coming! The Nazis are coming!"

"What?" we shrieked, and we all raced up the slope and looked, the smaller ones taking turns on Philip's back.

Far, far down on the valley road two green spots with helmets moved toward us on bicycles.

We looked at one another, terrified. Then I don't know how, but Henry, Arthur, Denise, and I, we all said at once, "The cave!" And we ran toward the back of the house. The others followed us.

Henry said to all of us, "No time for explanations. The four of us here know about a cave. Arthur, do you think you can find it again all by yourself?"

"Yes," said Arthur quietly and firmly.

"All right," said Henry. "Then you, the Jewish boys and and girls, go with Arthur and hide in the cave, and stay there, and do everything Arthur tells you to do. And wait—" He ran inside the house and came back with an empty pitcher and gave it to Arthur. "Take this and fill it with water at the stream, for drinking. Nobody knows how long you will all have to stay hidden."

Arthur said briefly, "Thanks. No matter what happens, we won't budge from the cave until one of you comes to give us the all-clear signal. Let's go."

The Jewish children moved right along. They did not make any fuss. They did not ask questions. They were used to danger. It took less time for them to disappear than it takes to tell it.

When they were gone Henry spoke up, "Now, listen, all of you. The hunt is on. Within half an hour the Nazis will be here. They are going to ask questions. We cannot betray. If we do, the Jewish boys and girls will be taken away, and we know the rest. So I suggest we play dumb. We just don't answer. Not a thing. Not even good day. Do you understand? We don't speak. Not one word. Not one word."

We all said, "That's right. We don't speak. Not one word. Not *one* word."

Then we went back to the front part of the yard. There

· 46 ·

was no use climbing on Philip's shoulders any more. The Nazis were plainly in sight.

Henry looked more upset than I had ever seen him before. "I wish Sister Gabriel were here," he kept saying to me. I ran inside the house, looked at the clock, and came back. "It's nearly five o'clock now," I said. "She cannot be long. She should be here any minute."

Henry shook his head. "If she were," he answered, "we could already see her on the road. It looks bad."

"Let's play," I suggested.

"What?" asked Henry gloomily.

"Leapfrog," I said. It was Henry's favorite game outside of make-believe.

"All right. Come on, all of you," called Henry "We're going to play leapfrog. All of us."

And so it was that when the two Nazi soldiers came into the yard, pushing their bicycles in front of them up the slope, we were leaping over one another at an ever-increasing speed in an unending line.

"Good day, children," said the soldiers in perfect French.

We all stopped playing but did not answer. We just looked at them.

"Good day. Can't you answer?"

Silence.

"Are you mute and deaf?"

Silence.

"My, it was a hard climb!" said one of the soldiers. "Am I thirsty! Any water around here, children?"

No answer.

"Come on, you pretty little girl, won't you show a soldier where to get a drink?" And one of the soldiers extended his hand toward Denise and caressed her cheek. Abruptly Denise sat down on the ground. We all laughed. That was a big mistake because it made the soldiers mad.

"All right," the one who looked rather young said sharply. "We will take care of you all later. Come on," he said to the other soldier, "we don't need them. We can search the house alone."

In they went, and we all sat down on the grass. There was nothing else to do. We heard them going all over the house. We knew they could not find anything, because the Jewish children had only the clothes they wore on their backs, and as far as beds were concerned, we shared them also, and the two blankets each one of us had.

Philip bent his head near the ground and whispered, "It's lucky we ate the thirty pieces of bread and the apples right away." It certainly was, or else the Nazis would have known for sure that ten of us were hiding somewhere.

Presently the soldiers came back and they made a sign for us to go inside. We did, and they waited until we were all seated. Then the young one, who seemed to be in command, said, "Children, we don't want to be mean to you.

But you have to answer us. Don't you have other children with you? Just say yes or no."

Dead silence.

"Why don't you answer? We are your friends, really. Are there some Jewish children with you?"

Not a word from the twenty of us.

"You nasty brats," bellowed the soldier. "I know how to make you talk."

A shiver ran through me, and I glanced out the window, hoping to see Sister Gabriel's white headdress coming up the path. But the road was deserted, and dusk was falling.

"It's no use looking out the window to see if your teacher is coming," I heard the soldier say, and I knew he was speaking to me. "Your teacher has been caught. She is in prison. So you see, you had better talk."

Sister Gabriel in prison! I recalled the young man's phrase: "You could be shot for this." As I opened my mouth in horror, my foot was stepped on ruthlessly. It was Denise, sitting next to me. That foot said, "Pretend! Pretend! Fool them!" I understood, and I made myself look like an idiot.

"That one looks stupid," said the soldier who was older.

"She certainly does," meanly the other soldier guffawed. "Better try this one. He looks bright." He meant Henry. "Come here, boy! You! Yes, you!"

Henry got up and went forward slowly.

"Now," said the young soldier, "you tell us where the

Jewish children are. If you don't, you will be sorry. No one is against us who is smart. Now speak up, or else—"

Henry stood there facing the Nazis in silence.

"Take him away," the young soldier ordered the other one, "and do as I told you."

The other soldier took Henry by the shoulders and pushed him out of the room. Henry managed to throw a glance at us. He was very pale; his fists were clenched, his lips tight, and in his eyes we read, "Hold on!" The door closed behind them. I wanted to shriek, "Henry! Henry!" But I dug my nails into my hands instead.

"See what happens to bad children!" said the young Nazi. "Now, boys and girls, don't be so foolish. Tell the truth. I am going to stay right here with you until one of you speaks up. I am in no hurry. I can wait all day, all night, forever."

He put his feet up on a chair, drew a pipe out of his pocket, lighted it, and puffed away. The clock ticked: tock, tick, tock . . . endlessly. And we sat there with our mouths closed, hardly daring to move. I'm sure we were all thinking of Sister Gabriel, the Jewish children, the cave, Henry, and wishing it were all over. Pretty soon it was dark. The soldier did not turn on the electricity. He just sat there, and I think at one time he went to sleep, so quiet it was.

Then the other soldier came back, without Henry, and the young one asked, "Did he talk?" "No," said the other one. "You're no good," snapped the young one. "I should have taken charge of him. Didn't you give him plenty?" "Plenty," said the other one.

All this was said in German, and only George could understand, because his parents are Alsatians, and he told us later what the Nazis had said. It was very hard on George that he did understand at the time, and he cannot be blamed for starting to cry. We didn't know why he did it, but we all felt so miserable that others joined him. Presently you could hear sobs all over the room.

The Nazis got up and yelled, "To bed! To bed! *Schnell! Schnell!* No supper. You did not talk. To bed! *Schnell!*"

So up we went and slipped into our beds, and I guess most of us cried ourselves to sleep. I did too, so I was very startled when I felt the pressure of a hand on my shoulder. I opened my eyes, and in the dark I faintly saw a familiar figure leaning over me. It was Henry!

He quickly put his hand over my mouth and whispered, "Listen. I got out. *He* put me in the coalshed. He's not quite so mean as the younger one. He's the old guard, the kind that fought in the First World War."

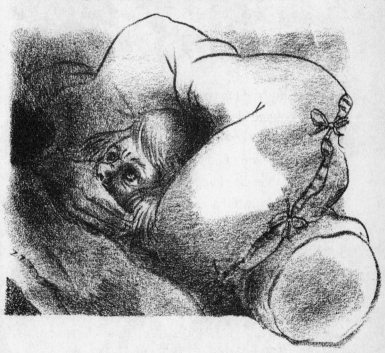

"What did he do to you?"

"He shook me like a plum tree, saying all the while, 'I'm going to thrash you within an inch of your life and then we will see if you won't find your tongue!' When we got to the coalshed he threw me in and locked me up. I heard his foot-steps going up the hill, and I was so afraid those in the cave would make a noise and he would discover them."

"How did you get out?"

"My good Scout knife. I cut a small piece out of a plank in the door, very neatly. Then I slipped my hand through and found that the key was right in the lock."

"Wonderful! Did you go to the cave?"

"No. I didn't dare. I didn't know where the Nazis were, and I figured out that if they came to look for me and didn't find me in the coalshed, it would be better for them to see me coming out of the house and not search for me in the hills. But listen, Janet, one of us has to go to the cave now and tell the others what is happening, or else they might wonder and come out and be caught. Besides, they must be cold and hungry."

"We're hungry too. We've had no supper," I said.

"Well, I didn't either," said Henry. "But we have to get some bread over to them now. There's no telling how long this will last."

"Where are the Nazis now?" I asked.

"Asleep on the sofa in the front room. So you see this is our chance." He paused, then, "Janet, would you mind going?"

I felt cold all over, but I asked quietly, "With you?"

"No," he said. "Because, as I told you, if I'm not in the coalshed, that might make matters worse. You go with Philip."

"Why Philip?"

"Because he's big and can carry four blankets easily. He could go alone if he knew where the cave is. But he doesn't. So that's why you have to go along. And you can carry two loaves of bread too."

I said, "Suppose *they* counted the loaves already?"

"Perhaps they did," said Henry. "Let's hope not. Anyway, they might think we ate them while they were asleep. Are you ready?"

Swallowing hard, I said, "Yes."

"Good," said Henry. "You get dressed, go down the back way, and get out the side door, the way I'm going now. You creep along the wall of the house, very quietly—better carry your shoes because of the noise of the wooden soles on the gravel—until you come to the boys' dormitory. Then stand under that window. Philip will throw you the blankets, and he will jump down, because for him it is not too high and he can get a foothold on the wisteria."

"What about the bread?"

"I'll get it when I go down now and leave it outside, under the boys' dormitory window. Ready?"

I said, "Suppose *they* wake up when you go to the kitchen?"

"I have to take a chance. Those in the cave have to eat."

"Suppose," I said again, "*they* wake up later and catch us, Philip and me—"

"Suppose, suppose!" retorted Henry impatiently. "If you don't want to go, say so. I'll ask Denise."

Was I mad! But I kept my peace. Henry seemed so nervous. Nevertheless, what a relief when he added, "It's all fixed, Miss Suppose. George is to hang a white handkerchief at the boys' window. It will remain there as long as the coast is clear."

I bit my lips not to interrupt with, "And if . . ."

Luckily Henry went on, "If you don't see the hanky, watch out. It means *they* are roaming abroad. And if *they* are, I have no suggestion. Use your wits. The only watchword: no matter what happens, no matter the cost, don't betray. All set?"

"Yes," I said firmly. I didn't want to hear the name of Denise mentioned again! But as Henry got up he gave me a friendly sharp poke in the ribs with his elbow, and I felt ready to face all the Nazis in the world.

There is not much to say about our getting to the cave. It went like clockwork. I got dressed, went down the back way, holding my shoes in my hand, got out the side door and crept along the wall barefooted, and no sooner had I reached the boys' dormitory window than four blankets came down on my head, one after the other. Before I had disentangled myself, Philip had slipped down. He was barefooted and had not bothered to take his shoes. We picked up everything, including the two loaves of bread, which were right where Henry said he would put them, and, waving good-by to George, who was tying the hanky at the window and was to remain on watch all the while, we skipped across the yard. Then I put my shoes back on, and in no time at all we were at the cave.

Philip stretched flat on the ground. He put his head in the crack and called softly, "Arthur!" At once we heard Arthur's voice, "Yes, Philip," very softly too. We handed the blankets down, and the bread, and then we ourselves slipped down.

At first we couldn't see anyone. But as our eyes got accustomed to the dark we saw the whole group huddled together at the far end of the cave, where it was the warmest. Were they happy to have the blankets!

Arthur said quietly, and as if he were not nervous at all, "The boys have been taking turns at watching. It's my turn now. That's why I was so near the entrance when you came. I heard you coming up. I knew right away that it was you and not the soldiers. And I knew too by the footsteps that there was a girl." He added quite sternly, "Why didn't Henry come? Why did he let a girl get into this jam?"

So we had to tell him everything that had happened, how Henry had to stay in the coalshed, and I had to show Philip the way.

Then Arthur told us they had heard the footsteps of the Nazi soldier coming up the hill. And he had sat right on the boulder above the cave for a long time, and they could smell the smoke of his pipe.

While Arthur talked he broke one of the loaves of bread in two. He went on, "We don't know how long before we see you again. We have to save as much as possible." Then he broke separate small pieces and handed them around, and he gave Philip and me a piece too, and we would not take it of course. But Arthur said, "If you don't eat, I won't either." And as we knew how determined and obstinate he could be, we had to eat. And did it taste good!

Philip told everyone, "We will be right over as soon as *they* are gone." And Arthur repeated, "No matter what happens, we won't budge from here until one of you comes to fetch us."

Then we had to leave. The whole group stood around us in the dark. All of us were so terribly afraid of being caught. But we did not speak about it. We just hugged and kissed one another over and over again.

Cautiously Philip and I crept out. We went stealthily down from bush to bush and behind rocks. Finally, there was the house, in the middle of the yard, and, thank God, the hanky was still floating at the window. I took off my shoes.

Philip said, "I'll go across first—alone. You stay hidden here. If everything is all right and you see me going up the wisteria, shoot across too, and crawl along the wall as you did before, and get back through the side door."

"All right," I whispered, my eyes on George's hanky up there.

Philip made a dash across. I saw him starting to climb

the wisteria, and I shot across too, but, as I did, off went the hanky. I crashed against the wall. I heard the side door open and shut and four heavy boots on the gravel. Flat against the wall, panic-stricken in the dark, I knew I was caught if

I did not think fast. As the beam of a flashlight pierced the night I quickly put my shoes back on and slowly, boldly, walked right out in the yard in the direction of the john, just as if I had come out of the front door. The voice of the young soldier cracked the air. "Stop, or I shoot!" At the same time the flashlight revolved and rested on me. I stopped. He came across quickly, followed by the other soldier.

"Only that stupid little girl of this afternoon," he said in a disgusted voice, and all in French, for my benefit, I suppose. "What are you doing out here at this time of the night? Spying, eh? I'll teach you!"

He grabbed me roughly by the arm and pushed me toward the side door. Heavens, I didn't want him to start questioning me! So I struggled like mad, pointing to the john all the time.

The old soldier said, "She probably was just going to the john."

"Well, ask her," said the young Nazi. "See if you can get more out of a girl than you did from that boy."

At once I started to yell.

"Shut up!" bawled the young soldier, dropping me like a hot potato.

Whereupon I ran full speed to the john. And there I stayed quite a time, and when I came out I walked proudly right in the open, past the Nazis who were talking. Dawn had come. I went upstairs and tumbled into bed, at last.

# 5. The Horrible-Day Miracle

I overslept—I guess we all did. I was awakened suddenly by the noise of bicycles on the gravel. I jumped out of bed and rushed to the window. I couldn't believe my eyes: the two Nazis were going down the slope on their bicycles. They were leaving!

I called everybody, and in no time we were all at the windows, watching them. They never so much as turned their heads back. We were so happy that we started dancing on the beds and throwing pillows at one another. Finally Philip said, "Let's go up to the cave and get the others." We all clapped, especially those who had never seen the cave. "Let's go! Let's go!" we cried.

"Oh, no!" said a voice. It was Henry's. We all stopped short, and we were ashamed because in all the excitement we had forgotten him in the coalshed. Then we started to laugh. We couldn't help it. He was black all over. In the dark I hadn't noticed it.

He said dryly, "Have fun! Have fun! No one thinks of coming to tell me I can get out. But you make enough noise for those in the cave to feel they can come out. And then they will be caught."

"Caught!" we said, gasping. We stepped down from the beds quietly. Someone said, "But, Henry, the Nazis have gone. We saw them go, way down the valley road."

"You have no sense," retorted Henry. "Let's hope the others in the cave have more than you have. I know they have, or else they would be here already."

Then Louis started to cry, "Sister Gabriel! Sister Gabriel!"

That sobered us completely, and we listened attentively to Henry as he went on, "Their leaving this morning like this, it's a trap, a trick. They want to see what we're going to do. They want to surprise us. They want to snatch our secret. They went, but they will be back. How do you know they aren't on their way back right now, cross-country? They're going to hide and spy on us. That's why we can't even go and say 'Hello' to the others in the cave."

Nobody had anything to say. We all had the creeps.

After a while Philip ventured, "Let's go down and eat."

That was a brilliant suggestion. It made us all feel much better. We went down, and Philip told how Arthur had divided the bread in the cave, and we all agreed to do the same and to save as much as possible in the way of food, because we didn't know how long it would have to last. So we girls cooked rutabagas, and we all had that and a small piece of bread each.

I don't know how we lived through that day. It was horrible. We kept feeling that *they* were watching us, and yet we didn't know if *they* were. We didn't dare even to throw a glance in the direction of the cave, and we lived in constant fear that those in the cave might get tired and, hearing nothing, come out.

In the afternoon someone suggested that we play at throwing rings. So we formed two teams, and we started to play, facing the road. It was my turn to throw, and I went over to take my place. I could see the road was deserted. I took the ring, and everybody was looking at me—that is, they had their backs to the road. I swung my arm and threw the ring, and everybody shrieked with terror as the ring was caught in mid-air by a man's arm which had shot up behind me. It was the young Nazi, who had sprung from around the corner of the house.

He laughed nastily. "Thought we were gone, eh? Didn't know we've been watching you for hours?"

We shuddered. Henry had been right.

"We've been looking around too," went on the Nazi. "We were told there are caves around this countryside. Don't you know about them, children? Let us go inside, we can talk better. Inside! Inside! *Schnell! Schnell!*"

Heavyhearted, we dragged our wooden shoes up to the house. The old soldier came in, carrying a large cardboard box. "Open it," ordered the young Nazi. While this was being done he said, "You did not have much to eat at noon. Rutabagas! I saw the peels in the garbage can. Poor children! Wouldn't you like a little extra? Look!"

He pointed to the box, out of which the old soldier proceeded to take out chocolate bars and colored candy. Our eyes popped, and we began to shift on our benches. But when the old soldier brought out oranges, real oranges, we couldn't help it: we shrieked. It was unbelievable. We had not seen oranges for years. Louis did not remember them at all—he was much too small—so he became very excited and clapped his hands, calling, "Pretty ball! Pretty ball for Louis!"

We were aghast. Up to this time Louis had been so good. He just had paid no attention at all to the Nazis. Of course he did not have the slightest idea of what was going on, but he had fallen in with the rest of us, naturally acting as we did. And now this!

The young Nazi was delighted. "Good! Good!" he said. "Come down here, little boy."

Denise snatched Louis and held him tight in her arms.

"All right," said the Nazi. "Then you both come."

So Denise had to get up. Carrying Louis, whose hand was stretched toward the oranges, she went up to the Nazi.

"Yes, little boy," he said, "you can have that pretty ball if you just tell me what I want to know. Now be a good little boy and tell me: don't you have some Jewish friends?"

"I forbid you to annoy my little brother!" yelled Denise.

"Oh yeah?" mocked the Nazi. "How funny! How very funny! You forbid me! And you talk, don't you? Better and better. Now we are getting somewhere."

Deliberately he took Louis away from Denise and sat him on his lap. "Go and sit down," he ordered Denise, who went back to her seat, crying. Then he spoke to Louis. "Listen carefully, little boy. You tell me the truth, and you can have the pretty ball, and the chocolate, and the candy. And all the others in the room can have it too. Tell me the truth. Don't you have some Jewish friends, boys and girls? Just say yes or no."

"Yes," said Louis.

In the hushed silence that followed, Henry got up slowly and said, "He does not understand. He is just trying to get the orange." Then I knew that Henry was playing the last card. Would it work?

"Did you hear?" the Nazi asked Louis, and he laughed. "It is not true of course. You know very well what I am talking about, don't you?"

Louis nodded triumphantly. I felt I was getting sick to my stomach.

"Of course!" rejoiced the Nazi. "You are a big boy! You know about Jewish boys and girls. Now tell me: where are they?"

"There!" said Louis at once, and he pointed to George, and me, and himself.

For a fraction of a second I was thunderstruck. Then I understood. Bless his heart! Louis remembered The Flight into Egypt and that George and I had held him. And, of course, we were the Jews.

"Pretty ball! Pretty ball!" Louis was demanding his due, but the Nazi seemed utterly dazed. He narrowed his eyes and peered from George to me, muttering, "Incredible! The nerve! Better even than I thought! Right here all the time!" Suddenly he shouted at George, "Get up! You!"

George got up. My heart was in my mouth. Had he understood?

"What's your name?" yelled the Nazi.

"Joseph," said George. Just like that. It was magnificent. I could have kissed him.

"And yours?" snarled the Nazi to me.

"Mary," I said.

"Fantastic!" sputtered the Nazi, wiping his forehead. And suddenly, as if waking up, he pushed Louis quickly off his knees with disgust and bellowed, "And what is *your* name?"

"Jesus!" shouted Louis proudly.

The whole room burst out laughing as the stunned Nazi opened his mouth wide. His eyes popped out and his arms fell to his sides. Then he caught sight of Louis walking toward the oranges. "Everything back in the box," he barked to the other soldier. But we did not care. Nothing could stop us from laughing. We roared. We shook all over. We shrieked. We cat-called. We hissed. The boys started to turn cartwheels in the aisles, and we girls threw ourselves on the floor and rolled all over.

Suddenly there was the sharp crack of a gun. We scrambled to our feet in a hurry, and there, in the doorway, stood a Nazi officer holding the gun he had fired into the air. And, next to him, was Sister Gabriel, very pale, anxiously taking the whole room in at a glance. In her eyes we read the burning question: "Where are our ten Jewish children?" And we could only look at her.

The officer said sharply, "Sister, are these your charges?"

"Yes," answered Sister Gabriel.

"Very badly brought up," snapped the Nazi officer. He turned to the young soldier. "Anything to report?"

"No, sir," said the young Nazi, red as a beet. Together

with the other, he had been standing at stiff attention since the officer had come in.

"Where are the Jewish children?" asked the officer.

"No Jewish children have been found, sir, except those three," said the young Nazi, snarling and pointing to George, Louis, and me. "Those three Jews whose names are Jesus, Mary, Joseph, so they say, the impudent brats, and—"

"Oh, but, sir," interrupted Sister Gabriel hurriedly with a gay little light in her eyes, "let me explain. It's a game the children play, The Flight into Egypt. You know, when Jesus' family had to flee because Herod's soldiers were hunting—" She stopped short. She was very red.

The officer did not seem to hear her. He barked to the young Nazi, "You have made a fool of yourself! A fool! Away with you! Report at once to the Normandy front. That will teach you."

The soldier clicked his heels and went out.

"You," said the officer to the other, "you come with me."

The officer clicked his heels, saluted Sister Gabriel, and recited like an automaton, "I am sorry for the inconvenience. You shall not be disturbed again. My advice, though, is that you give your charges a little taste of German discipline. They need it." He glared at us ferociously and then went out.

We crowded around the door. In the yard was a motor-cycle with a side seat in which the officer sat down, while the old soldier drove him. There was also a truck with three

SS troopers. Our tormentor, the young Nazi soldier, put his bicycle in the truck, next to that of the old soldier, and climbed in. There were some sharp commands, and down they went at top speed.

At last Sister Gabriel turned to us. "Where are they?"

And we all were still so afraid that we told her the whole story in whispers.

She kept laughing softly and saying, "Good! Good! Very good!" Then she said, "The Nazis arrested me as I went into Dieulefit. They had come back unexpectedly, and they questioned me. Of course I would not answer, so they threw me in jail. This morning they told me that they had sent two men up here, and that the Jewish children had been found. But still I would not talk. I figured out that perhaps they were lying, though I could not see how they could help catching the children. They said, 'You don't believe us? We'll take you back to the school now, and you will watch the Jewish children being taken away in that truck.' That was the truck you saw," added Sister Gabriel.

We all shuddered. Then Denise asked, "Do you think, Sister, that it is safe now, if one of us goes to the cave and tells the others that the coast is clear?"

"By all means," said Sister Gabriel. "Show me the way, Denise. I'll go with you."

Off they went.

After a while Suzanne appeared. We hugged her. "Where

are the others?" we asked. "Arthur says," she answered, "only one of us at a time, so it cannot possibly attract attention—just in case."

It took a little while for everybody to come down. Arthur was last. He said, "I think we should sleep in the cave from now on. During the day we can spell each other and keep a watch. But not so during the night. So it is best we sleep in the cave."

"He is right," said Sister Gabriel.

And that is the way it was done for the duration. During the day we were all together, and we took turns watching the road and the hills. At night the Jewish children went to the cave and stayed there until one of us went up in the morning to tell them it was safe to come out. We did have several bad scares later, and right during the night too, so it was fortunate that Arthur's plan had been followed. But nothing was so terrible as that first time. And when the Americans liberated the country the thirty of us were safe and sound, though the "sound" was somewhat hollow because we were all a little thin.

But to go back to that first time. We were all talking together and telling one another what had happened in the house and in the cave while the Nazis were on their hunt. Sister Gabriel said, "You were all very brave. I don't know which was the hardest: to face the Nazis or to stay hidden in the cave."

Suzanne said, "It seemed so long, so long! We did not dare talk, not even in whispers. We did not dare move. I tried to imagine that I was Mary for good and hiding in a cave on my way to Egypt. But Louis, the little one, was not there, and Arthur would not be Joseph—"

Arthur grinned. "Sister, I've had enough of The Flight into Egypt."

"So have I," said George. "Let's play something else. Couldn't we have a miracle, such as they played in the Middle Ages?"

"We could act out the multiplication of loaves and fishes," volunteered Philip, thinking of food as usual. But weren't we all thinking of it, all the time, in those days?

"That reminds me," said Sister Gabriel, "that *they* did not let me take any of the food packages at Dieulefit. So it means that we shall have to manage with the little we have to eat at present."

What a heavy blow! We had looked forward to those packages so much, and especially now we wished for them more than ever, after the Nazi scare. So we felt pretty blue.

Then Denise spoke up, "We can pretend. That is, we can act out the multiplication of loaves and fishes as Philip suggested, and do *just as if* we were eating."

Henry got up at once, all excited. He is a born director and stage manager. Already he was right in the play. "Let's all go out and sit on the grass," he said.

We did.

"Now," went on Henry, "we all are the common people, the great Jewish crowd which has come to hear Him. And He has told us such beautiful stories, and we like Him so much, that we stay and stay and stay—"

"We have been here for ages!" broke in Arthur.

"Indeed!" said Henry. "And now it is very late, and we all are so, so hungry—"

"So, so hungry!" we all chanted.

"And there is nothing to eat," went on Henry.

"Nothing to eat!" we all sang mournfully.

"Just a few—" started Henry.

And then we heard shrill cries, and we looked quickly toward where they came from. On the threshold of the house stood Louis. We had not noticed that he had slipped away. And there he was, shrieking at the top of his voice, "Pretty ball! Pretty ball!" and, in his hands, he waved— an orange!

One leap and a shout carried us all, including Sister Gabriel, to the house.

"Where, where did you find it, Louis?"

Triumphantly Louis led us. There, under the desk, was the forgotten Nazi box filled with chocolate, candy, and oranges!

Was there ever, ever, a sweeter miracle?

## ABOUT THE AUTHOR

Claire Huchet Bishop grew up in Le Havre, France. Her grandfather was the village storyteller, and in the winter evenings people would gather around his fire. Her mother, too, was a dramatic storyteller, and so it was only natural that after Claire finished her studies at the Sorbonne and began working at the first French Children's Library in Paris she should begin telling stories there.

When she married an American and moved to New York, she began to write down her stories, as well as telling them at the New York Public Library. Besides *Twenty and Ten*, she is the author of *The Man Who Lost His Head* and *Twenty-Two Bears*—all books which stem directly from her storytelling experience.